The Night After Christmas

by JAMES STEVENSON

Copyright © 1981 by James Stevenson. All rights reserved. This edition published by Scholastic Book Services, a division of Scholastic Inc., 730 Broadway, New York, NY 10003, by arrangement with Greenwillow Books, a division of William Morrow & Company, Inc.

12 11 10 9 8 7 6 5 4 3 2 1   11   2 3 4 5 6/8
Printed in the U.S.A.   07

SCHOLASTIC BOOK SERVICES
NEW YORK · TORONTO · LONDON · AUCKLAND · SYDNEY · TOKYO

It was the night after Christmas. Teddy was in the garbage.
"Jingle bells, Jingle bells," he sang. "Jingle all the way…"

"Why are you singing?" said a doll who was in the garbage next door.
"I don't know," said Teddy. "It's better than *not* singing."
"So you got thrown out, too?" said the doll.
"Sure did," said Teddy. "The kid who owned me got a space gun
for Christmas."

"My name is Annie," said the doll.
"I'm Teddy," said Teddy.
"Merry Christmas, Teddy," said Annie.
"Same to you, Annie," said Teddy.

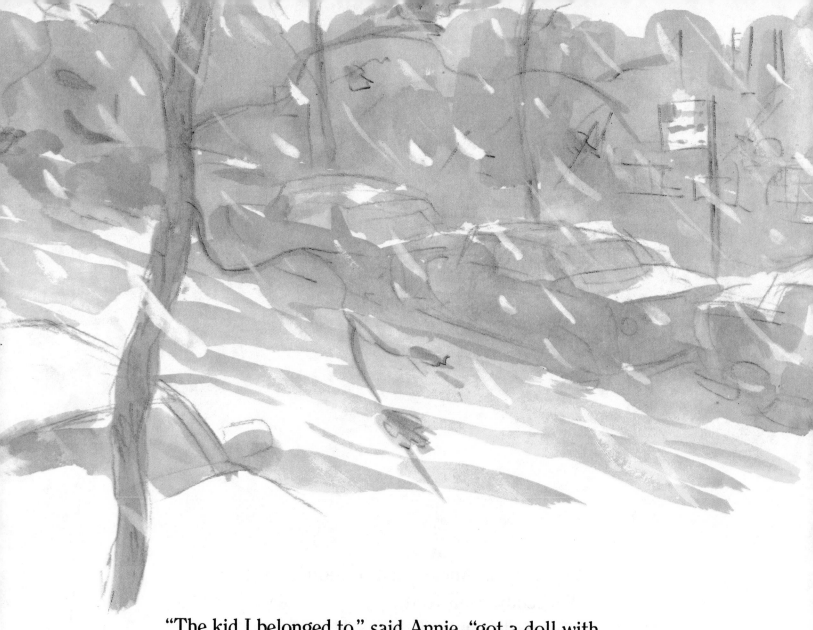

"The kid I belonged to," said Annie, "got a doll with
hair you can curl and clothes you can change plus a bikini."

"Want to sing 'Jingle Bells'?" said Teddy.
"Not right now," said Annie.

"A word to the wise," said a voice. "They collect the garbage here first thing in the morning." It was a brown dog.

"Where can we go?" asked Annie.
"You can come to my place," said the dog.
"Thank you," said Teddy.
"Climb aboard," said the dog. "My name's Chauncey."

"It's not fancy," said Chauncey, "but it's warm."

They all went to sleep.

In the morning, Teddy said, "What do we do now?
There's nobody to play with."
"I'll play with you," said Chauncey.
"Thanks," said Teddy, "but I meant children."

"Nothing personal, Chauncey," said Annie.
"That's O.K." said Chauncey. "I'm not much for games anyway.
I run, bark, and wag my tail. That's about it."
Chauncey went out to hunt up some breakfast.

"You know what we should do?" said Teddy.

"What?" said Annie.

"We should fix ourselves up as new toys," said Teddy. "The kind kids want."

"I am what I am," said Annie. "I can't be anything else."

"Well, I can," said Teddy. "I could be on television.
Kids love that."
"No you couldn't," said Annie.
"You'll see," said Teddy. "Clap if you like it."

Teddy climbed into a box.
"Everybody in the whole family loves Yummy!"
said Teddy. "Tell Mom to buy the large size today!
It's nourishing and delicious!"

"You didn't clap," said Teddy.
"I didn't like it that much," said Annie.
"I have a better idea," said Teddy.
 He went away for a moment.

"What are you supposed to be?" said Annie.
"I am a toy computer," said Teddy.
"Ask me a question."
"How can you be so stupid?" said Annie.
"Is that the question?" said Teddy.

"What now?" said Annie.
"Don't you know a creature from outer space
when you see one?" asked Teddy.

Chauncey came back.
"Having a good time?" he asked.
"No," said Teddy.
"Far from it," said Annie.
"Oh, well," said Chauncey. "You'll get used to it."

For the next few days, Teddy and Annie just sat around,
feeling sadder and sadder.

Teddy began to pace back and forth, back and forth.
"What's the problem?" asked Chauncey.
"I can't get used to getting used to it," said Teddy.

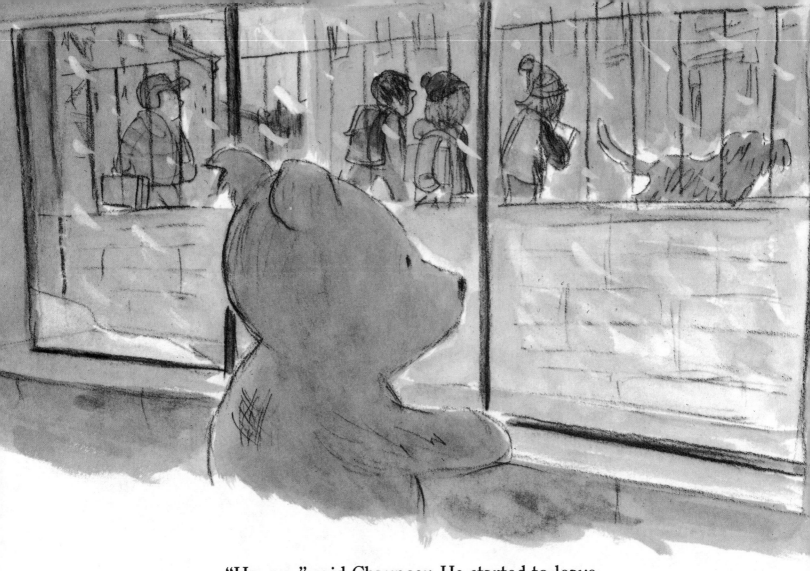

"Hmmm," said Chauncey. He started to leave.
"Where are you going?" said Annie.
"Can we come, too?" said Teddy.
"No," said Chauncey. He was gone a long time.

When Chauncey came back, he wouldn't tell them where he'd been. "You'll find out tomorrow," he said.

The next day he took them down the street.
"Wait till you see," he said.

They stopped at a big building.
"What's so special?" asked Annie.

"You sit there, Annie," said Chauncey, "and you sit there, Teddy."
"I hear a bell ringing," said Annie.

Suddenly, children began pouring out of the doors.

They made a lot of noise, and it took a long time.

When all the children were gone,

Annie and Teddy were gone, too.

The End